The Hound of the Baskervilles

According to
Spike Milligan

TED SMART

This edition produced for
The Book People Ltd
Hall Wood Avenue, Haydock
St. Helens WA11 9UL

First published in hardback in Great Britain
in 1998 by Virgin Publishing Ltd

Reprinted 2003

Illustrations by Rob Seabury

A catalogue record for this book is available from
the British Library

ISBN 0 7535 0927 X

Typeset by Galleon Typesetting, Ipswich
Printed and bound by Mackays of Chatham

Contents

The Hound
of the
Baskervilles

Foreword

Sherlock Holmes was hurled to his death by Professor Moriarty but his death did not last long. He climbed up a thousand-foot mountain and killed Moriarty, who later became a character in *The Goon Show*.

CHAPTER I

𝕸𝖗 𝕾𝖍𝖊𝖗𝖑𝖔𝖈𝖐 𝕳𝖔𝖑𝖒𝖊𝖘

SHERLOCK HOLMES usually arrived brilliantly very late in the morning; his record for lateness was not coming down until the next morning. As we sat eating breakfast at 3 a.m., I stood upon the hearthrug and picked up the stick which our visitor had left behind the night before. It was a fine, thick piece of wood with a bulbous head known as a brain smasher. Just under the head was a broad silver band inscribed 'To James Mortimer, MRCS, from his friends of the CCH', with the date '1884'. It was just such a stick as murderers or old family practitioners used to carry – dignified, solid, and bloody heavy.

'Well, Watson, what would you make of it?'

'Firewood,' I said.

Holmes was sitting with his back to me and I had given him no signs of my occupation.

'Now what is your occupation, Watson?'

'I am a Coastal Spotter.'

'And what is that?'

'Well, I'm a Coastal Spotter. You go to the coast, you spot things and you report them to the Coast Guard.'

'And do you spot anything unusual?'

'Yes, I saw a man starving on a raft.'

'And what did the Coast Guard do?'

'They shot him.'

'Isn't that murder, Watson?'

'Not on the high seas,' said I. 'Spotting in Japanese is Yamaguchi. I did Yamaguchi for two years. I spotted a pirate ship and the Coast Guard sank it by gunfire. As the pirates swam ashore, the Japanese police drowned them by putting rocks in their clothes.'

'It seems, Watson, that the Coast Guard is hellbent on eliminating the human race.'

'Well, there do seem a lot of them.'

'Tell me, Watson, what do you make of our visitor's stick, since we have been so unfortunate as to miss him?'

'I think,' said I, analysing the implement as best I could using the methods of Holmes, 'that Mortimer is a successful elderly medical man, well esteemed – since those who know him gave him this stick as a mark of their appreciation.'

'Good!' said Holmes. 'Excellent! Ten out of ten!'

'Now this stick would seem to be the property of an elderly man,' I added.

'You know, Watson, you are a genius and have a remarkable power of stimulation. I must confess, my dear fellow, that I am very much in your debt.'

'Well, I would be grateful if you would start paying it off.'

He lit a cigarette, which flared up and set fire to his shirt front, which I doused with a soda siphon.

The doorbell had gone.

4

'Do come in,' cried Holmes.

The appearance of our visitor was a surprise to me since I had expected a typical country practitioner. He was a very tall, thin man, with a toothless dog by his side.

'Good morning,' said Holmes.

As he entered his eyes fell upon the stick in Holmes's hand, and he ran towards it with an exclamation of joy.

'Whooee! Whooee!' he said. 'I am so very glad,' said he. 'I was not sure whether I had left it here or in the Shipping Office. I would not lose that stick for the world.'

'Ah, a presentation, I see,' said Holmes.

'Yes, sir. From one or two friends at Charing Cross Hospital on the occasion of my marriage.'

'Pardon me, do I understand you received a walking stick as a wedding present?'

'Yes.'

'I am sorry but, if you will pardon me, what a crappy present. I got a toast rack.'

'Ah yes,' said Mortimer, 'but you can't take a toast rack for a walk.'

'Nonsense! I take my toast rack for a walk in the country. I took it to the Himalayas and made toast on K2 at twenty-two thousand feet and it worked perfectly.'

'I presume that it is Mr Sherlock Holmes whom I am addressing and not –'

'No, that is my friend Dr Watson. I am here near the window.'

'Good heavens!' said Mortimer. 'You're not going to jump out, are you?'

'As he entered his eyes fell upon the stick in Holmes's hand, and he ran towards it with an exclamation of joy.'

'Not yet. It depends on you.'

'Oh, I am glad to see you, sir. I have heard your name mentioned in connection with that of your friend. You interest me very much. I hardly expected so dolichocephalic a skull or such well-marked supraorbital development. Would you have any objections to my running my finger along your parietal fissure?'

'Look here, man,' said Holmes. 'You leave my parietal fissure alone! It's bad enough to have one.'

'My dear Holmes, as you wish, but a cast of your skull, until the original is available, would be an ornament to any anthropological museum. It is not my intention to be fulsome, but I must confess that I covet your skull.'

'No! No! Don't covet my bloody skull! It's bad enough just having one!' Sherlock Holmes waved at the visitor. 'Have a chair.'

'No, I'll stand.'

'All right, then bloody well stand on the chair.'

'You are an enthusiast in your line of thought, I perceive, sir, as I am in mine,' said Mortimer.

Holmes was silent, but his little darting glances showed me the interest which he took in our curious companion.

'I presume,' said Mortimer, 'that your little darting glances show an interest in me.'

'I presume,' said Holmes, 'it was not merely for the purpose of examining my skull that you have done me the honour to call here?'

'No, sir, but I am happy to have the opportunity of doing that as well. Mr Holmes, because I recognise myself that I am an impractical man who cannot tie my shoelaces nor roll a cigarette and because I am suddenly confronted with a most extraordinary problem, and recognising, as I do, that you are the second highest expert in Europe –'

'What, sir! May I enquire who has the honour to be the first?' said Holmes, his face white with anger.

'To the man of precisely scientific mind the work of Monsieur Bertillon must always appeal strongly.'

'All right, then, you had better consult him, and bugger off! And that will be ten guineas!'

'It is acknowledged that you stand alone.'

'At the moment I have insufficient funds to stand a loan,' said Holmes quickly. 'My fee is ten guineas an hour with a down payment of one hundred guineas.'

At the mention of a fee Dr Mortimer fainted and was revived only by pouring a bucket of water over him and extracting the money from his pocket.

'It came to pass that one Michaelmas the shit, with five or six of his idle and wicked companions, stole a maiden.'

CHAPTER II

The Curse of the Baskervilles

'I HAVE IN my pocket a manuscript,' said Dr James Mortimer.

'Of course you have. I observed it as you entered the room,' said Holmes. 'It was sticking out a mile. It is an early-eighteenth-century one.'

'How can you say that, sir?'

'Never mind how I said it; I said it.'

'Good heavens! The exact date is 1742. It was committed to my care by Sir Charles Baskerville, whose sudden and tragic death three months ago created so much excitement in Devonshire. I must say that I was his personal friend as well as his medical attendant.'

'Well, as he's dead, your practice doesn't seem to be very successful,' said I.

'Oh, what have we here?' said Holmes and Mortimer proceeded to read from the document.

' "As to the origin of the Hound of the Baskervilles, there have been very many statements. I come in a direct line from Hugo Baskerville. He was wanton and cruel but there was in him a certain wanton and cruel humour which made him known as the shit.

"It came to pass that one Michaelmas the shit, with five or six of his idle and wicked companions, stole a maiden. When they had brought her to the Hall the maiden was placed in an upper chamber while the shit and his friends sat down to a long carouse. Now, the poor lass, at her wits' end, slid down the ivy, tore her crotch to pieces, but escaped to freedom.

"It chanced later that the shit left his guests to carry food and drink to his captive and so found the cage empty and the bird escaped; whereupon the shit ran around the house crying to his grooms to saddle his mare and unkennel the pack of hounds, who had been brought up on jam, so in full cry they set off for the jam factory.

"Alas, there in the clearing lay the unhappy maid where she had fallen, dead of fear and of fatigue. But it was not the sight of her body, nor yet was it that of the body of the shit lying near her, which raised the hair upon the heads of those who discovered them." Are you still listening?' said Dr Mortimer.

'Just,' replied Holmes.

' "It was that, standing over the shit, and plucking at his throat, there stood a foul thing, a great, black beast, shaped like a hound yet larger than any hound any mortal eye had seen. It tore the throat out of the shit. As it turned its blazing eyes and dripping jaws upon them they all shrieked with fear." Well,' said Mortimer, 'did you find it interesting?'

'To a collector of fairy tales,' scoffed Holmes.

Dr Mortimer drew a folded newspaper out of his pocket.

'Now, Mr Holmes, we will give you something a little more recent.'

'Well, hurry up. It's my wedding anniversary in two days.'

'This is the *Devon County Chronicle* of June the fourteenth of this year. It is an account of the facts elicited at the death of Sir Charles Baskerville.'

Quack! Quack!

'Watson, stop that duck!'

Our visitor readjusted his glasses and began:

' "His health was sometimes impaired. He had a heart disease that changed his colour – one day he was red, the next day he was green-striped and then a light primrose colour. He was breathless sometimes. There was no need to be: there were tons of fresh air. All he had to do was suck it in." '

'Is there much more of this?' asked Holmes, yawning.

'The facts of the case are simple. On the fourth of June Sir Charles was starting next day for London, and had ordered Barrymore to prepare his luggage, a billiard table, a gas stove, a blow-up female doll, and a puncture kit. That night he went out as usual for his nocturnal walk. He never returned. At twelve o'clock his body was discovered.'

'Was he dead?' I asked.

'Yes, thank God. I thought he was going to go on for ever.'

'Oh, very interesting,' said Holmes, 'but what has this got to do with me?'

Quack! Quack!

'Stop that duck!' cried Holmes.

Dr Mortimer refolded his paper and replaced it in his trousers. It went straight through into his sock as he had no lining in his pocket. He leant back, put his fingertips together but, alas, he had been using superglue and they were stuck there.

'I must thank you,' said Holmes, 'for calling my attention to a case which certainly presents some features of interest. I had observed some newspaper comment at the time. This article, you say, contains all the public facts?'

'It does.'

'Then let me have the private ones.'

'In doing so,' said the boor Dr Mortimer, who had begun to show signs of some strong emotion, 'I am telling that which I have not confided to anyone. My motive for withholding it from the coroner's inquiry is that a man of science shrinks from placing himself in the public position of seeming to endorse a popular superstition.'

Any minute now Sherlock Holmes was going to tell him to bugger off!

'You wouldn't like to bugger off, would you?' said Holmes to Dr Mortimer.

'I can well remember driving up to the house in the evening, some three weeks before the fatal event. He chanced to be at his hall door. I descended from my gig and was standing in front of him, when I saw his eyes fix themselves over my shoulder and stare past me with an expression of the most dreadful horror.

' "The Baskerville hound!" he shrieked.

'I looked around in time to see a gigantic something, which I took to be a large black calf passing at the head of the drive. So excited and alarmed was he that I was compelled to go down to the spot where the animal had been and look around for it and there it was – gone.'

'Your claim to fame is that you saw the Hound of the Baskervilles?' mused Holmes.

'Sir Charles' heart was affected, and the constant anxiety in which he lived, however chimerical the cause of it might be, was having a serious effect upon his health.'

'Please stop,' said Holmes.

'On the night of his death Barrymore said there were no traces –'

'Oh my God, he's going on.'

'– of footsteps except those of Sir Charles. He said that there were no traces upon the ground near the body. He did not observe any. But I did – some little distance off, but fresh and clear.'

'Footsteps?' said Holmes.

'Footprints.'

'A man's or a woman's?'

Dr Mortimer looked strangely at us for an instant, and his voice sank to a whisper as he answered, 'Mr Holmes, they were the footprints of a gigantic hound!'

'Oh fuck,' said Holmes.

'Dr Mortimer looked strangely at us for an instant, and his voice sank to a whisper as he answered, "Mr Holmes, they were the footprints of a gigantic hound!"'

CHAPTER III

The Problem

I CONFESS THAT at these words a shudder passed through me and out the back. Holmes leant forward in his excitement and his eyes had that hard, dry glitter which shot from them when he was keenly interested.

'You saw this thing?'

'As clearly as I see you.'

'And you said nothing?'

'Yes, I said, "Look at that fucking thing!"'

'How was it that no one else saw it?'

'No one else was there. The marks were some twenty yards from the body.'

'How can a dog race twenty yards and kill somebody? You say it was large?'

'Enormous.'

'What sort of night was it?'

'Like every night – dark. Please don't ask silly questions.'

'But not actually raining?'

'No, he wasn't raining.'

Holmes was very thorough with his questioning.

'Was he wearing a hat?'

'No, I was.'

'There are two lines of old yew hedge, twelve feet high and impenetrable.'

'Where is all of this getting us?' asked Mortimer.

'I understand that the yew hedge is penetrated at one point by a gate?'

Oh brilliant questioning, Holmes, brilliant!

'Had Sir Charles reached this gate?'

'No, he lay about fifty yards from it.'

'Are you saying he travelled fifty yards after he was dead?'

'Yes, he was a very strong man.'

'How high was this gate?'

'About ten feet.'

'Could anyone have got over it?'

'Only if he was an Olympic hurdler.'

'What marks did you see?'

'In fact the wicket gate had been bitten in half by a giant dog.'

'There is a realm in which the most acute and most experienced of detectives is helpless,' said Holmes.

'You mean that thing is supernatural?' I asked.

'There was one clue,' said Mortimer. 'There was a pile of dog crap three feet high.'

'One dog?'

'Yes, sir, one dog.'

'Couldn't several dogs have done it in concert?'

'No one does such a thing at a concert.'

'I will have to make a note of that,' said Holmes.

'I don't care if you make a sandwich of it,' said Mortimer.

'Tell me in the same breath that it is useless to investigate Sir Charles's death and that you desire me not to do it.'

'I did not say that I desire you to do it.'

'My fee is ten guineas an hour and one hundred guineas deposit.'

The doctor made a dash for the door but I managed to intercept him and made him pay up.

'The current Sir Henry Baskerville is arriving from Canada at Paddington Station,' said Holmes. 'I recommend, sir, that you take a cab, call off your spaniel, who is scratching at my front door, kick him up the arse, and proceed to Paddington Station to meet Sir Henry. You will say nothing to him at all until I have made up my mind about the matter.'

'How long will it take you to make up your mind?'

'Twenty-four hours. At ten o'clock tomorrow, Dr Mortimer, I will be much obliged to you if you will call upon me here; that's a chance you'll have to take, and it will be of help to me in my plans for the future if you will bring Sir Henry Baskerville with you and a cheque for one hundred guineas.'

At the mention of the money, Mortimer again tried to escape from the room.

'One more question, Dr Mortimer. You say that before Sir Charles Baskerville's death several people saw this apparition upon the moor?'

'Three people did.'

'Did any see it after?'

'No, only during.'

* * *

I went to the Turkish bath at the club and lost two stone in the steam bath and my wallet.

Holmes suffered hours of intense mental concentration during which he weighed every particle of evidence – it gave him a nosebleed – constructed alternative theories, balanced one against the other, and made up his mind which points were essential and which were immaterial. Clever sod, but expensive.

'Where do you think I've been, Watson? I have been to Devonshire.'

'In spirit?'

'Exactly. My body remained in this armchair – it saved train fare.'

He would do anything to save train fare. He was a mean bastard: we called him glue pockets. Once he put his hands in them he never took them out.

'After you left I sent down to Stanford's for the Ordnance Survey map. I flatter myself that I can find my way about. If I was any flatter I would disappear. The devil's agents may be of flesh and blood, may they not?'

'Well, that goes for most people except the Hindus, who don't have blood, only curry.'

'If Dr Mortimer's surmise should be correct, we are dealing with forces of evil.'

'Oh, how do you do it, Holmes?' Actually he did it like everybody else.

'Yes, I have thought a good deal of it in the course of the day. What do *you* make of it?'

'I would make a rice pudding of it.'

'He was running, Watson – running desperately,

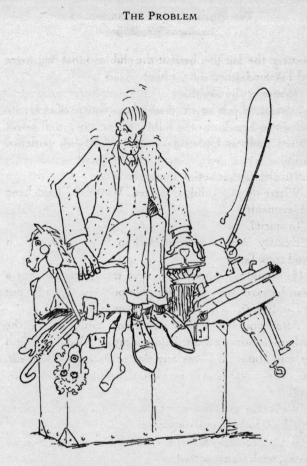

*'Everything was packed for his journey to London —
the hobby horse, the grand piano, billiard table and
blow-up rubber doll with puncture outfit.'*

running for his life, running until he burst his heart and fell face down on his back, dead.'

'How can you say that?'

'It's easy. I just say it. Everything was packed for his journey to London – the hobby horse, the grand piano, billiard table and blow-up rubber doll with puncture outfit.'

'He's done that before, hasn't he?'

'... *"Do take a seat."*
"No, I'll stand."
"All right, then stand on a bloody seat." '

CHAPTER IV

Sir Henry Baskerville

OUR CLIENTS were punctual to their appointments. The clock was just striking ten and Dr Mortimer was one of them. He was followed by the young baronet, sturdily built, thick black eyebrows and a strong, pugnacious face. He had the weather-beaten appearance of one who spent most of the time in the open air or drowning.

'This is Sir Henry Baskerville,' said Dr Mortimer.

'Pleased to meet you,' said Holmes. 'Do take a seat.'

'No, I'll stand.'

'All right, then stand on a bloody seat. Do I understand you to say that you have had some remarkable experience since you arrived in London?'

'Nothing of much importance, Mr Holmes. Only a joke, as like as not.'

He laid an envelope upon the table. 'It was this letter, which reads, "As you value your life or your reason keep away from the moor." ' It was printed in ink. 'Now,' added Sir Henry, 'you will tell me what in thunder you make of it.'

'I would make sponge pudding out of it.'

'As far as I can follow, Mr Holmes,' said Sir Henry, 'someone cut out this message with scissors.'

'*The Times* is a paper seldom found in any hands but those of the highly educated. We may take it, therefore, that the letter was composed by an educated man in black wearing a white tie and tails, a cape, silk top hat, patent-leather boots and a thousand pounds in loose change. Did the composer fear an interruption – and from whom? Mrs Doris Stokes.'

'Mrs *Doris Stokes??!!!*'

'Now you would call it a guess, no doubt, but I am certain that this address has been written in an hotel,' said Holmes.

'How in the world can you say that?' asked Sir Henry.

'I just can. I am bloody brilliant. Sir Henry, has anything else of interest happened to you?'

'No, Mr Holmes, I think not. Only the loss of a boot. I don't know much of British life yet, for I have spent nearly all my time in Canada counting moose. But I hope that to lose one of your new brown boots is not part of the ordinary routine of life over here.'

'You have lost one of your boots?'

'My dear sir,' cried Dr Mortimer, 'it is only mislaid. You will find it when you return to the hotel.'

'Perhaps,' said Holmes, 'but this event gives us food for thought, no matter how foolish the incident may seem. Left or right?'

'I don't know until I find it,' said Sir Henry.

'Look, Sir Henry,' said Holmes, 'I'll be willing to wear the odd boot until you find the other one.'

'It seems an unusual thing to steal unless the thief is one-legged,' I observed.

'It may be that they wish for their own purposes to scare me away and they left me with one boot so I couldn't travel to Baskerville Hall.'

'There seems to be danger,' muttered Holmes.

'Do you mean danger from human beings?'

'Are there any other kind? It's something *out there*!' said Holmes, pointing upward. 'Meanwhile I have hardly had time to think over all that you have told me. It's a big thing for a man to decide at one sitting. I should like to have a quiet hour by myself to make up my mind.'

'Suppose you and your friend, Dr Watson, come around and lunch with us at two?' suggested Sir Henry.

'Is that convenient to you, Watson?' enquired Holmes.

'I can't. I have a brain operation at three.'

'Yes? What's wrong with your brain?' asked Holmes.

'It's coming apart.'

'I'll join you and your one boot with pleasure,' said Holmes.

'Then we meet again at two o'clock. Au revoir, and good morning!' Sir Henry waved goodbye, opened the door and walked into a cupboard, came out again and left via the front door with Mortimer in tow.

'Quick, Watson, quick! Not a moment to lose!'

Holmes rushed into his room, collided with a bus, and was back again in a few seconds. We hurried down the stairs together and into the street, where we collided with a bus. Dr Mortimer and Baskerville were still visible about two hundred yards ahead of us.

At that instant I saw a hansom cab with a man inside who got out when it halted on the other side of the street and then walked slowly onward towards Mortimer and Sir Henry.

'There's our man, Watson! Come along! We'll have a good look at him, if we can do no more.'

But the man leapt back into the cab and at that instant I was aware of a bushy black beard and a pair of piercing eyes turned upon us through the side window of the cab. Instantly the trapdoor at the top flew up, something was screamed to the driver, and the cab flew madly off down Regent Street. Holmes looked eagerly round for another, but none were going cheap. Then he dashed in wild pursuit amid the stream of traffic and collided with a bus. But the start was too great and already the cab was out of sight and Holmes was knackered. He had to rest, so he lay down on the pavement and went to sleep.

'Watson, you are an honest man. You will record this also and set it against my successes!'

'Who was the man?'

'I have no idea.'

'Was it a spy?'

'Well, it was evident from what we heard that Baskerville has been very closely shadowed by someone since he has been in town. Whoever it was may have actually stolen the lost boot to stop him travelling anywhere. You may have observed that I twice strolled over to the window.'

'You weren't considering jumping out?'

'As it is, our eagerness was taken advantage of with extraordinary quickness and energy by our opponent.

We have betrayed ourselves and lost our opponent.'

'Fuck!'

We had been sauntering slowly down Regent Street during this conversation, and Dr Mortimer, with his companion, had long vanished in front of us.

'There is no object in our following them or we will vanish as well,' observed my companion.

'I could only swear to the beard,' I said.

'In all probability it was a false one. A clever man upon so delicate an errand has no use for a beard save to conceal his teeth. Come in here, Watson!'

We turned into one of the district messenger offices, where he was warmly greeted by the manager.

'Ah, Wilson, I see you have not forgotten the little case in which I had the good fortune to help you?' said Holmes.

'No, sir, indeed I have not. You saved my good name, and perhaps my life.'

'We all make mistakes, son,' said Holmes. 'I have some recollection, Wilson, that you had among your boys a bright lad called Cartwright, who showed some ability during the investigation. Could you ring him up? Thank you. I should be glad to have change of this five-pound note.'

A fourteen-year-old lad with a bright visage, keen face held together with pimples, had obeyed the summons of the manager.

'Let me have the *Hotel Directory*,' said Holmes. 'Now, Cartwright, there are the names of twenty-three hotels here, all in the immediate neighbourhood of Charing Cross. Do you see?'

'Yes, sir.'

'You will visit each of these in turn.'

Twenty-three hotels! Was he mad?!

'You will begin in each case by giving the outside porter one shilling. Here are twenty-three shillings.'

He *is* bloody mad!

'You will tell him that you want to see the wastepaper of yesterday. You will say that an important telegram has miscarried, and that you are looking for it. You understand?'

He ought to be in a straitjacket under supervision!!

'But what you are looking for is the centre page of *The Times* with some holes cut in it with scissors. Here is a copy of *The Times*. It is this page. You can easily recognise it, can you not?'

'Yes.'

'You will then learn in possibly twenty cases out of the twenty-three that the waste of the day before has been burnt or removed. In the three other cases you will be shown a heap of paper, and will look for this page of *The Times* among it. The odds are enormously against your finding it.'

Why did he bother to send the lad?

Thus passed another lunatic idea of Holmes.

'Sherlock Holmes had, in a very remarkable degree, the power of detaching his mind at will.'

CHAPTER V

Three Broken Threads

SHERLOCK HOLMES had, in a very remarkable degree, the power of detaching his mind at will. He removed it and placed it on the mantelpiece in the lobby of the hotel where we were to meet with Baskerville and Mortimer.

'Have you any objection to my looking at your hotel register?' Holmes asked the porter.

'Not in the least, sir.'

The book showed that two names had been added after that of Baskerville. One was Theophilus Johnson and family of Newcastle; the other Mrs Oldmore and maid, of High Lodge, Alton.

'Surely that must be the same Johnson whom I used to know,' said Holmes to the porter. 'A lawyer, is he not, grey-headed, and walks with a limp?'

'You're wrong, sir. This is Mr Johnson, the coal-owner, a very active gentleman, not older than yourself, and does not limp.'

'Surely you are mistaken.'

'Wrong, sir. He has used this hotel for many years, and he is very well known to me.'

'Mrs Oldmore, too; I seem to remember the name –

a very keen horsewoman and showjumper.'

'She is an invalid lady, sir, and never goes anywhere.'

So much for the brilliance of Mr Sherlock Holmes's identification ability.

'What's the matter, Holmes?' I asked.

'No stranger has checked in after Mortimer and Baskerville,' said Holmes. 'Whoever is stalking them is not in residence here.'

As we came round the top of the stairs we ran up against Sir Henry Baskerville himself. His body and face were flushed with anger as were several of his fingers.

'It seems to me they are playing me for a sucker in this hotel,' he cried. 'If that chap can't find my black boot I will shoot a policeman.'

'But surely, you said that it was a new brown boot?' said Holmes.

'So it was, sir. And now it's a new black one.'

'Do make up your mind – black or brown?'

'When they stole my brown one, I bought a black pair; now that is missing.'

'Look,' said Holmes, 'I am only too proud to wear your brown and now your black one until they are found.'

An agitated German waiter had appeared on the scene.

'You German *Schweinhund*!' said Holmes. 'You and your nation are preparing for World War One – now get out and do it. Well, either that boot comes back before sundown, or I'll alert the Grenadier Guards.'

'It shall be found, sir – I promise you that,' he said,

doing a Nazi salute and goosestepping out the door as Dr Mortimer arrived.

Holmes asked Baskerville what his intentions were.

'To go to Baskerville Hall.'

'On the whole,' said Holmes, 'I think that your decision is a wise one. Did you know that you were followed this morning from my house?'

Dr Mortimer started violently. 'Followed! By whom?'

'That, unfortunately, is what I cannot tell you.'

'Oh fuck!' said Mortimer.

'Have you among your neighbours or acquaintances on Dartmoor any man with a black, full beard?'

'Why, yes. Barrymore, Sir Charles's butler, is a man with a full, black beard.'

'Ha! Where is this Barrymore?'

'Ha! He is in charge of the building. He is charged with not letting it fall down.'

'We had best ascertain if he is really there. Give me a telegraph form. We can write "Is all ready for Sir Henry?", address it to Mr Barrymore, Baskerville Hall, and we will say, "Are you there?" '

The devilish cunning of Sherlock Holmes never ceased to amaze me.

'Now, Dr Mortimer,' said Holmes. 'Tell me all you know of this Barrymore.'

'So far as I know, he and his wife are as respectable a couple as any in the country.'

'Did Barrymore profit at all by Sir Charles's will?' asked Holmes.

'I hope,' said the boor Dr Mortimer, 'that you do not

look with suspicious eyes upon everyone who received a legacy from Sir Charles, for I also had a thousand pounds left to me.'

'Indeed! While he was blowing it all, how much did he leave?'

'A great deal. There were many insignificant sums to individuals and a large number of public charities. He left ten thousand pounds to the Berlin Philharmonic Orchestra.'

'And how much was the residue?'

'Seven hundred and forty thousand pounds.'

Holmes raised his eyebrows and went green with envy. 'I had no idea that so gigantic a sum was involved,' said he.

'Sir Charles had the reputation of being rich. The total value of the estate was close on to a million.'

'Dear me! It is a stake for which a man might play a desperate game, like Arsenal versus Spurs. Supposing that anything happened to our young friend here, who would inherit the estate?'

'The widows of the Arsenal and Spurs football match. There are distant cousins, so distant you can hardly see them. James Desmond is an elderly clergyman in Westmorland. He came to visit Sir Charles. He is a man of venerable appearance and of saintly life. I remember that he refused to accept any settlement from Sir Charles, though he pressed and pressed him until he was much thinner and finally grabbed the money and ran from the room screaming "RICH, RICH, RICH".'

'Quite so. Well, Sir Henry, I am of one mind with you as to the advisability of your going without delay. There

'There were many insignificant sums to individuals and a large
number of public charities. He left ten thousand pounds to the
Berlin Philharmonic Orchestra.'

is only one provision which I must make. You certainly must not go alone.'

'Dr Mortimer returns with me.'

'No, Sir Henry, you must take with you someone, a trusty man, who will always be by your side.'

'Is it possible you come yourself, Mr Holmes?'

'No, I will stay behind and wear your boots. You can buy a new pair. It will be my honour to wear your old ones.'

'Whom would you recommend then?'

Holmes laid his hand upon my arm. 'If my friend would undertake it there is no man who is better worth having at your side when you are in a tight place.'

'Well, now, that is real kind of you, Dr Watson,' said Sir Henry. 'Then on Saturday, unless you hear to the contrary, we shall meet at the ten-thirty train from Paddington. Would that suit Dr Watson?'

We had risen to depart when Baskerville gave a cry of triumph, and diving into one of the corners of the room he drew a brown boot from under a cabinet. 'What a pity,' he said, 'I threw the other one away. You can still wear one black one and one brown one.'

'Look,' said Holmes, 'I am willing to wear the remaining odd boots until you buy another pair. It is not often I am honoured by being allowed to wear any of the Knights of the Realm's boots.'

The German was sent for and the very appearance of him enraged Sherlock Holmes.

'You *Schweinhund mit Krieg kommen Sie mir! Dummkopf!* Herr Fritz, I accuse you of spying for and working for the German Government and hiding Allied boots to prevent them from marching to war. *Schweinhund* and fuck the Kaiser.'

The German gave the Nazi salute.

Just before dinner two telegrams were handed in. The first ran:

> HAVE JUST HEARD THAT BARRYMORE IS AT
> THE HALL.
>   BASKERVILLE.

The second one:

> YOU BASTARD, HOLMES, WHY DID YOU SEND
> ME ON A WILD-GOOSE CHASE.
>   CARTWRIGHT.

'That's funny,' said Holmes. 'I don't remember sending him on a wild-goose chase. I wonder if he caught any?'

'We have still traced the cabman who drove the spy,' I reminded him.

Holmes decided to question the cabman immediately.

'First of all your name and address, in case I want you again.'

'James Clayton.'

'I will make a note of it.'

'I don't care if you make a Dundee cake out of it.'

'And now, Clayton, before I make a Dundee cake, tell me about the fare who came and watched this house at ten o'clock this morning.'

'The truth is that the gentleman told me that he was a detective and that I was to say nothing about him to anyone.'

'Did this detective mention his name?'

'He said his name was Sherlock Holmes.'

Holmes burst into a hearty laugh. 'For all I know I might be Florence Nightingale. How would you describe Sherlock Holmes?'

'He wore a beard which completely concealed his teeth.'

'Nothing more you can remember?'

'Oh yes, I remember it's my wife's birthday.'

'Well, then, here is your half-sovereign.'

John Clayton departed downstairs chuckling, and Holmes turned to me with a shrug of the shoulders and a rueful smile.

'Bloody working class,' said Holmes and spat out of the window in time for it to alight on Clayton's head.

'I am sending you on an ugly business, Watson, ugly, dangerous and the more I see of it the less I like it. God knows what horrors await you.'

Quack! Quack!

'Stop that duck!'

'Mr Sherlock Holmes drove me to the station – he didn't have a carriage; he had a whip.'

CHAPTER VI

Baskerville Hall

MR SHERLOCK Holmes drove me to the station – he didn't have a carriage; he had a whip.

'You can leave me to give orders,' he said.

'What orders? Would it not be well in the first place to get rid of this Barrymore couple?' I suggested.

'By no means. It would be a cruel injustice. No, no, we will preserve them upon our list of suspects. Then there is a groom at the Hall, if I remember right. There are two moorland farmers. There is our friend Dr Mortimer, whom I believe to be entirely honest, and there is his wife, of whom we know nothing. There is a naturalist Stapleton and his sister. These are the folk who must be your very special study.'

'I will do my best, Holmes.'

'But we can't afford failure, Watson. You have arms, I suppose?'

'Yes, and legs.'

'Keep your revolver near you night and day and never relax your precautions. And, if anybody attacks you, escape by shooting yourself and make a getaway.'

'Take one of them every night with water.' I handed him an illegible prescription.

Our friends had already secured a first-class carriage and were waiting for the train to be late.

'We have no news of any kind,' said Dr Mortimer.

Good God, he was still with us!

'We have never gone out without keeping a sharp watch, and no one could have escaped my notice,' said Dr Mortimer.

'You have always kept together, I presume?'

'Yes, I always kept together and so did Sir Henry. He kept together.'

'Dr Mortimer,' I said, 'avoid the moor in those hours of darkness when the powers of evil are exalted.'

'What a lot of balls,' said Sir Henry.

I looked back at the platform when we had left it far behind, and saw the tall, austere figure of Holmes standing motionless, gazing after us wearing one brown boot and one black and that absurd deerstalker hat.

The journey was a swift and pleasant one. I spent it playing with Dr Mortimer's spaniel. The little bastard bit me so I kicked his arse. Baskerville stared eagerly out of the window and cried aloud with delight as he recognised the familiar features of the Devon scenery.

'It is all as new to me as it is to Dr Watson, and I'm as keen as possible to see the moor,' said Sir Henry.

'Oh are you? Then your wish is easily granted, for there is your first sight of the moor,' said Dr Mortimer, pointing out of the carriage window.

'Oh,' said Sir Henry, 'is that all it does?'

Baskerville sat for a long time. It was his first sight of

'The journey was a swift and pleasant one. I spent it playing with Dr Mortimer's spaniel.'

this beautiful spot, which was about six inches in circumference. He sat there wearing one brown boot and one black one.

The train pulled up at a small wayside station and we all fell out. A wagonette with a pair of cobs was waiting. Percival was the driver. Our coming was evidently a great event.

'Three cheers for Sir Henry: hip, hip, hooray!' said the station master, and waved a green flag and blew a whistle for us. Unfortunately the driver didn't know it was a welcome whistle so the train started up and left the station.

It was a sweet, simple country spot. I was surprised to observe that by the gate there stood two soldierly men in dark uniforms who leant upon their short rifles. There was a convict at large on the moor. A few minutes and we were flying swiftly down the broad white road. Rolling pasture lands curved upward on either side of us.

'Halloa,' cried Dr Mortimer. 'What is this?'

'This is England,' I said. 'I thought you knew.'

On a summit was a mounted soldier, his rifle poised over his forearm. He was watching the road along which we travelled.

'What is this, Percival?' asked Dr Mortimer.

'There's a convict escaped from Princetown, sir,' said Percival. 'He's been out three days now, and the warders watch every road and every station but they have had no sight of him. You see, he isn't like an ordinary convict.'

'What does an ordinary convict look like?'

'Oh, very ordinary. It is Selden, the Notting Hill murderer.'

'Oh, we must tell the villagers to watch out for a man called Selden, the Notting Hill murderer, and to stay awake with a pistol by your side. If he attacks, shoot yourself and your family before he can hurt you.'

Somewhere on that desolate plain was lurking this fiendish man, the Notting Hill murderer, hiding in a burrow like a wild beast. As if we didn't have enough trouble with this phantom hound.

'Baskerville Hall,' said Percival.

When we arrived, Sir Henry stepped down wearing odd boots. He was looking at the alterations made by his late ancestors and the improvements consisted of a Japanese golf course, a supermarket and a bingo hall, all with flashing lights. It cheered Sir Henry's Canadian soul to see the illuminations. He walked into a low branch, rendering himself unconscious.

'Welcome to Baskerville Hall, Sir Henry,' said a servant.

'You're bloody welcome to it too!' said the semi-conscious Sir Henry.

'Welcome, Sir Henry! Welcome to Baskerville Hall.'

A tall man had stepped from the shadow of the porch to open the door of the wagonette. It was Barrymore. A woman came out and helped the man to hand down our bags.

'You don't mind my driving straight home, Sir Henry?' said Dr Mortimer.

'*He walked into a low branch, rendering himself unconscious.*'

'My man, you would drive anybody home,' replied Sir Henry.

'My visiting fee is five pounds,' said the good doctor as a helpful reminder.

Sir Henry went to an early fridge. He opened it and took out a tin of 1889 lager and swallowed and immediately threw up.

'It's just as I imagined it,' said Sir Henry. 'Bloody awful. To think that this should be the very same hall in which for five hundred years my people have lived!'

Barrymore had returned from taking our luggage to our rooms. He stood in front of us now with the subdued manner of a well-trained servant. He was a remarkable-looking man, tall, handsome, with a square black beard and pale distinguished features. He looked as if he would die any moment.

'Would you wish dinner to be served at once, sir?'

'Is it ready?'

'Yes, are you? My wife and I will be happy to stay with you until you have made fresh arrangements, but you will understand that under the new conditions this house will require a considerable staff.'

'What are the new conditions?'

'We want more money.'

'Do you mean your wife and you wish to leave?'

I seemed to discern some signs of emotion on the butler's white face.

'I hope, sir, that you discern the signs of emotion on my white face. I feel very bad about this, sir, and so does my wife. I fear that we shall never again be easy in our minds at Baskerville Hall.'

'Then what do you intend to do?'

'Bugger off, sir. Have no doubt, sir, that we shall succeed in establishing ourselves in some business. Sir Charles's generosity has given us the means to do so. And now, sir, perhaps I should best show you to your freezing bloody rooms.'

Sir Henry kept walking into the wall. 'Isn't there a bloody light or a door along here somewhere?'

'Yes, you're leaning against it now.' Which he did, and forthwith catapulted into the room.

'My word, it isn't a very inviting or warm place,' said Sir Henry.

'Well, sir, you could set fire to it.'

'I don't wonder that my uncle got a little jumpy here.'

'Yes, he would jump all around the room until he was tired, then he would lie down, then would do some more jumping. He tried to enter for the Olympics but was too tired.'

We retired to our rooms late that evening. Suddenly, in the very dead of the night, there came a sound to my ears, clear, resonant and unmistakable. It was the sob of a woman, the muffled, strangled gasp of one who is torn with uncontrolled sorrow. What was he doing to her?

Dr Watson enjoys the warmest affections of the Barrymores.

CHAPTER VII

The Stapletons of Merripit House

THE MORNING did something to calm all our minds. As I sat at breakfast the sunlight flooded in through the high mullioned windows. That woman crying in the night had given me the shits.

'Did you hear a woman sobbing in the night?' I asked.

'Yes, I did. I waited quite a time but there was no more of it so I presumed he had stopped doing it to her,' replied Sir Henry.

'I heard it distinctly, and I am sure that it was really the sob of a woman.'

Sir Henry asked Barrymore whether he could account for our experience. It seemed to me that the pallid features of the butler turned a shade paler still as he listened to his master's question.

'There are only two women in the house, Sir Henry,' he answered. 'One is the scullery maid, who sleeps in the other wing. The other is my wife, and I can answer for it that the sound could not have come from her.'

I met Mrs Barrymore in the long corridor with the

sun full upon her face. She was a large, impassive, heavy-featured woman with a stern, set expression of mouth. But her telltale eyes were red and glanced at me from between swollen lids. It was she, then, who wept in the night. What had he been doing, the swine? Why had she wept so bitterly? Was the swine using a feather duster on her?

I decided to make enquiries at the local Post Office to establish whether Barrymore had been at the hall to receive the telegram Holmes had composed.

'Certainly, sir,' said the postmaster, 'I had the telegram delivered to Mr Barrymore exactly as directed.'

'Who delivered it?'

'My boy here. James, you delivered that telegram to Mr Barrymore at the Hall last week, did you not?'

'Yes, Father, I delivered it.'

'Into his own hands?' I asked.

'Well, he was up in the loft at the time, so that I could not put it into his own hands, but I gave it into Mrs Barrymore's hands.'

'Did you see Mr Barrymore?' I asked.

'No, sir; I told you he was in the loft.'

'If you didn't see him, how do you know he was in the loft?'

'Well, surely his own wife ought to know where he is,' said the postmaster testily. 'If there is any mistake it is for Mr Barrymore himself to complain.'

The conclusion was that Barrymore was working on a new appliance to use on his helpless wife.

Suddenly my thoughts were interrupted by the sound

of running feet behind me and a voice called my name. To my surprise, it was a stranger who was pursuing me. He was a small, slim, clean-shaven, prim-faced man, flaxen-haired and lean-jawed, between thirty and forty years of age, dressed in a grey suit and wearing a straw hat. A tin box for botanical specimens hung over his shoulder and he carried a green butterfly net.

'You will, I am sure, excuse my presumption, Dr Watson,' said he. 'You may possibly have heard my name from our mutual friend, Dr Mortimer. I am Stapleton, of Merripit House.'

'How did you know me?'

'I have been calling on Mortimer, and he pointed you out to me from the window of his surgery as you passed. We were all rather afraid that after the sad death of Sir Charles the new baronet might refuse to live here. It is asking much of a wealthy man to come down and bury himself.'

'Oh, he doesn't intend to bury himself. He intends to go on living above ground.'

'Of course, you know the legend of the fiend dog which haunts the family? I may be of some help to you in this strange matter.'

'You think, then, that some dog pursued Sir Charles, and that he died of fright in consequence?'

'Have you any better explanation?' asked he.

'Yes, an elephant fell on him.'

'And how about Mr Sherlock Holmes?'

'He brilliantly does not know. I assure you that I am simply here to visit my friend, Sir Henry, and I need no help of any kind. Now piss off!'

'You are perfectly right to be wary and discreet and I promise you that I will not mention the matter again.'

We came to a steep, boulder-sprinkled hill which had in bygone days been cut into a granite quarry. The face turned towards us on the dark cliff, with ferns and brambles growing in its niches. From over a distant rise there floated a grey plume of smoke. It was a perfect mantrap; it trapped me. I couldn't find my way out until dawn.

As Holmes had expressly said I should study the neighbours upon the moor, I accepted Stapleton's invitation to his home.

'It is a wonderful place, the moor,' he said, looking around in terror. 'A false step means death to man or beast. Only yesterday I saw one of the moor ponies wander into it. He never came out. I saw his head for quite a long time craning out of the boghole, but it sucked him down at last. The same thing happened to our postman. It sucked him down. The milkman was another victim. Before he was sucked down he said, "Play for me," so I played for him but he still got sucked down.

'The Mire has him,' Stapleton continued. 'Two in two days, and many more, perhaps, for they get in the way of going there in the dry weather and never know the difference until the Mire has them in its clutch. It's a bad place, the Great Grimpen Mire.'

'You say you can penetrate it?'

'Yes, with a thermos of tea and a packet of sandwiches. There are one or two paths which a very active man can take. I have found them out.'

'But why should you wish to go into so horrible a place?'

'Well, mainly for the tea and sandwiches. It's where the rare plants and the butterflies are if you want to reach them.'

'I'll try it one day.'

'For God's sake, put such an idea out of your mind,' said he. 'Your blood would be upon my head.'

'Oh? How would it get up there? Halloa,' I cried. 'What is that?'

A long, low moan, indescribably sad, swept over the moor. It filled the whole air, and yet it was impossible to say whence it came. From a dull murmur it swelled into a deep roar and then sank back again into a melancholy, throbbing murmur once more.

'Queer place, the moor!' said he. 'Queers haunt it day and night. The peasants say it is the queer Hound of Baskerville calling for its prey.'

'You're an educated man. You don't believe such nonsense as that?' said I. 'What do you think is the cause of so strange a sound?'

Quack! Quack!

'Why have you brought a duck?' Stapleton asked.

'For company,' I replied.

'Bogs make queer noises sometimes,' said Stapleton.

'Yes, I've used a few. No, no, that was a living voice.'

'Look at the mounds on the hillside yonder. What do you make of those?'

'I would use them as night soil,' I said.

'No, they are the homes of our worthy ancestors. Neolithic man, no date.'

'What did they do?'

'They grazed cattle on the slopes, they grew potatoes and killed each other so they soon ran out of people.'

A small butterfly crossed his path and in an instant Stapleton was rushing with extraordinary energy and speed in pursuit of it. To my delight the creature flew straight for the great Mire. If only it would suck him down.

A woman approached me and was certainly that, and of a most uncommon type. There could not have been a greater contrast between brother and sister. Stapleton was neutral-tinted, with light hair and grey eyes, while she was darker than any brunette whom I have seen in England – slim, elegant, and tall.

'Go back!' she said. 'Go straight back to London instantly.'

'Go back?' I said. 'I've only just got here. Why should I go back?'

'For heaven's sake, do what I ask you and never set foot upon the moor again.'

'Don't set foot on it? How are we going to get about?'

Stapleton had abandoned the chase, and came back to us breathing hard.

'You have introduced yourselves, I can see.'

'Yes,' said she. 'I was telling Sir Henry that it was rather late for him to see the true beauties of the moor.'

'Why, who do you imagine this is?'

'I imagine that it must be Sir Henry Baskerville.'

'No, no,' I informed her. 'I am only a humble commoner, but his friend. My name is Dr Watson.'

'Oh, I'll wash my hands.'

'*A small butterfly crossed his path and in an instant Stapleton was
rushing with extraordinary energy and speed in pursuit of it.*'

We went to Merripit House. Inside there were large rooms furnished with an elegance in which I seemed to recognise the taste of a lady. I broke a piece off and tasted it – it tasted of a lady.

'Queer spot to choose, is it not?' said he, pointing to a queer spot on the ground. 'I find an unlimited field of work here, and my sister is as devoted to Nature as I am. Every morning you see her dancing naked on the lawn.'

'It certainly did cross my mind that it might be a little dull – less for you, perhaps, than for your sister, which explains her Doric postural dancing.'

'No, no, I am never dull,' she said quickly. 'We have books, we have our studies, we have interesting neighbours, and we have fish and chips with Worcestershire sauce and McDonald's with milkshakes. Do you think that I should intrude if I were to call this afternoon and make the acquaintance of Sir Henry?'

'I am sure that he would be delighted.'

'I could show him my materials, miniature heads of Tutankhamen.'

'Oh yes, of course.'

But I was eager to get back to my charge. The melancholy of the moor, the death of the unfortunate pony, the postman, the milkman and the weird sound which had been associated with the grim legend of the Baskervilles and the queers on the moors – all these things tinged my thoughts with sadness.

On my way back I reached the road and was astounded to see Miss Stapleton sitting upon a rock by the side of a track. Her face was beautifully flushed with excitement and cheap scent.

'I have run all the way in order to cut you off, Dr Watson. I must not stop, or my brother may miss me. I wanted to say to you how sorry I am about the stupid mistake I made in thinking that you were Sir Henry. Please forget the words I said, which have no application whatever to you.'

'But I can't forget, Miss Stapleton. I am Sir Henry's friend and his welfare is a close concern of mine. Why were you so eager that Sir Henry should return to London?'

'A woman's whim, Dr Watson. When you know me better you will understand that I cannot always give reasons for what I say or do. I dance naked every morning on the grass with no reason but that I must. I felt I should warn him of the danger which he will run.'

'What is the danger?'

'You know the story of the hound?'

'I do not believe in such nonsense. Some people say it is the queer Hound of the Baskervilles. The world is wide, Miss Stapleton. In some places it is twelve feet by thirty feet.'

'I cannot say anything definite,' she said, 'for I do not know anything definite.'

She turned and disappeared in a few minutes among the scattered boulders, divesting herself of her clothes as she went.

Quack! Quack! Stop that duck!

The Grimpen Mire held many gruesome secrets, including the whereabouts of an unfortunate moor pony, the local postman and a wayward milkman.

CHAPTER VIII

First Report of Dr Watson

MY DEAR Holmes,
My previous letters have kept you pretty well up to date as to all that has occurred in this most godforsaken corner of the world but this is my first full report.

We are four able-bodied men in this household and we could take good care of ourselves. I sleep with a pistol under my pillow and every morning when I wake up it's still there. It is not to be wondered that time hangs heavy in this lonely spot. We hang it from a beam and it keeps good time.

Stapleton gives the idea of hidden fires. As yet we can't find where he hides them. He has the strange habit of drinking a glass of Horlicks before retiring.

He came over to call upon Baskerville and took us both to see the spot where the legend of the wicked Hugo, the shit, was supposed to have its origin. He pointed to a spot in the carpet.

'That's it,' he said. 'That's the spot where the wicked Hugo, the shit, was supposed to have its origin.'

We found a short valley between rugged High Tors. High Tor, I tort I saw a puddy tat but when I got there there was none. He really did believe in interference of the supernatural in the affairs of men. I told him I had never had an affair with men. He told us cases where families had suffered some evil influence – they all exploded and were never seen again. We asked him if he could tell us where they went. They went to bits.

From the moment Sir Henry saw Miss Stapleton he appeared to be strongly attracted, putting a great strain on his trousers. Such a match would be very welcome to Stapleton, yet I more than once caught a look of the strongest disapprobation on his face. As Sir Henry said more than once, when paying close attention to his sister, Stapleton had the look of strongest disapprobation on his face.

I cannot help but think of the old man, Sir Charles, as he stood there and saw something coming across the moor, something which terrified him so much that he lost his wits. There was a long, gloomy tunnel down which he fled and from what? Eh? A sheep dog of the moor? Eh? A spectral wild hound? Eh? A Notting Hill murderer? Eh? People said it was an Eric. An Eric? Eh?

One other neighbour I have met since I wrote last. This is Mr Frankland, of Lafter Hall. His passion is for the law, and he has spent a large fortune in litigation. He fights for the mere pleasure of fighting, especially against people of the parish. Sometimes he will shut up a right of way and defy the parish to make him open it.

And now, having brought you up to date in the escaped convict, the Stapletons, Dr Mortimer and Frankland of

Lafter Hall, the homosexual hound and Erics, let me tell you more about the Barrymores, and especially about the surprising developments of last night.

You are aware that I am not a very sound sleeper. Last night, about two in the morning, I was aroused by creaking footsteps. I opened my door. A long black shadow was trailing down the corridor. It was thrown by a man who walked softly down the passage with a candle in his hand. By piecing together his footsteps I realised he was doing the rhumba. He was in shirt and trousers, with no covering to his feet. It was Barrymore.

Barrymore crouched at the window with a candle held against the glass. His profile was half turned towards me, and his face seemed to be rigid with expectation as he stared out into the blackness of the moor. For some minutes he stood watching intently. Then he gave a deep groan, and with an impatient gesture he put out the light. Instantly, I made my way back to my room.

'. . . she put me on Coca-Cola. I'm on that three times a day.'

Chapter IX

The Light Upon the Moor

I ASKED BARRYMORE what he was on.

'Guinness and Newcastle Brown. I mainline it straight into the vein.'

'Can't you kick it?'

'No. I need a fix three times a day.'

'What does it do for you?'

'It gets me pissed.'

'Have you been to a psychiatrist?'

'Yes, she put me on Coca-Cola. I'm on that three times a day.'

Before breakfast on the morning following my adventure I went down the corridor and examined the room in which Barrymore had been the night before. I stood in the same place he had. The trouble is he was still standing there. It was all more than a little embarrassing.

I had an interview with Sir Henry in his study after breakfast and he was less surprised than I had expected.

'I see you are less surprised than I expected,' I said.

'I knew that Barrymore walked about nights, and I

had in mind to speak to him about it,' said he. 'I will do it together and you do it together. Two or three times I have heard his steps in the passage coming and going.'

'I am certain it was the rhumba,' I said.

'We must take our chance. What was his object with the rhumba?'

'Perhaps he pays a visit every night to that particular window,' I suggested.

Sir Henry rubbed his hands with pleasure and hand cream.

Sir Henry had been in communication with the architect who prepared the plans for Sir Charles, and with a contractor from London, and planned that great changes should begin soon. There had been decorators and furnishers up from Plymouth who painted Sir Henry green when the house was being renovated and refinished.

After our conversation Sir Henry put on his hat and prepared to go on the moor.

'What, are *you* coming, Watson?' he asked, looking at me in a curious way; that is, using his head back to front.

'It all depends whether you are going on the moor,' said I.

'Well, I am,' he said. 'I have to: the WC is broken so we have to use the moor.'

'Well, you know what my instructions are. I am sorry to intrude but you heard Holmes insist that I should not leave you here, and especially that you should not go on the moor.'

'But I have to. I am telling you that the WC is

broken.' Sir Henry put his hand on my shoulder with a smile. 'I am to meet Miss Stapleton on the moor.'

Our friend, Sir Henry, and the lady had halted on the path, and were standing deeply absorbed in their conversation when a wisp of green floating in the air caught my eye and another glance showed me that it was carried on a stick by a man who was moving along the broken ground. It was Stapleton with his butterfly net. He was very much closer to the pair than I was, and he appeared to be moving in their direction. At that moment I fell off the rock into a bog and I came up dripping with ooze and smelling like disinfectant. Stapleton put the net over my head and I said there must be some mistake: I was not a specimen.

At that instant Sir Henry suddenly drew Miss Stapleton to his side. His arm was round her but it seemed to me that she was straining away from him with her face averted. I watched from a distance as Stapleton tried to catch her in his butterfly net but she kept ducking behind Sir Henry. Sir Henry dodged as Stapleton lunged towards them, his net thrust out in front of him. He gesticulated and almost danced. He put his net over his sister's head and took her away.

'Hello, Watson,' said Baskerville. 'Where have you dropped from? Good God, you smell of shit!'

'It will wash off,' I said.

Quack! Quack! Stop that duck will you!

'You don't mean to say that you came after me in spite of all? You would have thought the middle of that prairie a fairly safe place for a man to be private,' said he, 'but, by thunder, the whole countryside seems to be out to see me do my wooing! Where had you engaged a seat?'

'I was on that hill clinging to a boulder.'

'Of course you were.'

'That fool put the net over my head and I said there must be some mistake: I am not a specimen.'

'Tell me straight now, Watson, is there anything that would prevent me from making a good husband to a woman that I loved? Her brother seems a lunatic. Is he of sound mind?'

'Yes, you can hear him a mile away.'

'Yes,' he said, 'he would not have me as much as touch the tips of her fingers. Listen, there's a light in a woman's eyes that speaks louder than words. In fact, I had to use ear plugs but he has never let us get together. She has never been together and I have never been together. She would not speak of love so I spoke to her of the bubonic plague in Rajputa. If he had not been her brother I would have known better how to answer him, the cunt. Just tell me what it all means, Watson. I'll owe you more than ever I can hope to pay.'

'No, sir, I am quite satisfied with a hundred guineas per day retainer.'

'I can't forget the look in his eyes when he ran at me this morning, but I must allow that no man could make a more handsome apology than he has done.'

'Did he give any explanation of his conduct?'

'Yes, he said he had piles and they were playing him up. I told him his arsehole has nothing to do with me. You do not use piles as an apology – it is a condition.

'He said he was a lonely man with only her as a

companion, so the thought of losing her was really terrible to him. Surely if he lost her he could look for her. He was very sorry for all that had passed. He himself was past fifty.'

I sat up with Sir Henry until three o'clock in the morning. One struck, and then two. We heard the creak of a step in the passage – strike three. We walked into the room and as we did Barrymore sprang up from the window with a sharp hiss of his breath, and stood, livid and trembling, before us.

'What are you doing here, Barrymore?' demanded Sir Henry.

'I was doing the rhumba, sir.'

'Come, come, that's not the rhumba; that's the carioca.'

'I swear, sir, I am doing nothing.'

'Rubbish! No one can do nothing.'

'Yes, you can, sir. You close your eyes, lie quite still and you stop breathing.'

A sudden idea occurred to me and I took the candle from the windowsill, where the butler had placed it.

'He must have been holding it as a signal,' said I. 'Let us see if there is any answer.'

I held the candle to my ear – there was no sound. Then I gave a cry of exultation, for a tiny pinpoint of yellow light had suddenly transfixed the dark veil, and glowed steadily in the centre of the black square framed by the window.

'There it is!' I cried.

'Move your light across the window, Watson!' cried

the baronet. 'See, the other moves also! Now, you rascal, do you deny that it is a signal? Come, speak up! Who is your confederate out yonder and what is this conspiracy that is going on?'

The man's face became openly defiant. 'It is my business, and not yours. I will not tell.'

'Then you will leave my employment right away.'

'Then that will be a little case of seven hundred and fifty quid back pay.'

'Right, there's one pound in advance,' said Sir Henry, the mean bugger.

'No, no, sir; no, not against you!'

It was a woman's voice, and Mrs Barrymore, white as paper and more horror-struck than her husband, was standing by the door. Her bulky figure in a shawl and skirt might have been comic were it not for the intensity of feeling upon her face.

'Oh, John, John, have I brought you to this? It is my doing, Sir Henry – my doing!'

'What about your doings?'

'My unhappy brother is starving on the moor. We cannot let him perish at our very gates.'

'Why not? It's as good a place as any.'

'The light is a signal to him that the food is ready for him, and his light out yonder is to show the spot to which to bring it.'

'Then your brother is . . .'

'Yes, the escaped convict, sir, Selden, the Notting Hill murderer.'

'That's the truth, sir,' said Barrymore. 'I said that it was not my secret, and that I could not tell it to you. But now you have heard it, and you will see that if there was a plot it was not against you.'

'So your brother is Selden, the Notting Hill murderer?'

'Yes, sir, my name was Selden, and he is my younger brother. We humoured him when he was a lad and gave him his own way in everything, until he came to think that the world was made for his pleasure and that he could do what he liked in it. Then he met wicked companions, and the devil entered into him, until he broke my mother's heart and dragged our name in the dirt. From crime to crime he sank lower and lower until he nearly disappeared. We took him in and fed him and cared for him. Then you returned, sir, and my brother felt he would be safer on the moor than in prison, or the police, or hanging.'

The woman's words came with an intense earnestness which carried conviction.

'Is this true, Barrymore?' asked Sir Henry.

'Yes, sir, every word of it.'

'Well, I cannot blame you for standing by your wife and candle and accept a rise in wages of sixpence.' (Mean swine.)

When they were gone the cold wind blew in and nearly froze our balls off. Far away in the black distance there still glowed that one tiny point of yellow light.

'It may be so placed as to be only visible from here,' said I.'

'Very likely. How far do you think it is?'

'It's out by the High Tor, I tort I saw a puddy tat. I will come,' said I.

'Then get your revolver and put on your boots. The

73

"Are you armed?" I asked. "I have a hunting crop and a mincer."

sooner we start the better, as the fellow may put out his light and be off.'

'Are you armed?' I asked.

'I have a hunting crop and a mincer.'

'Good! We must close in on him rapidly for he is said to be a desperate fellow. We must take him by surprise, kill him and then mince him.'

Suddenly out of the vast gloom of the moor came that strange cry which I had heard upon the borders of the Great Grimpen Mire. It came with the wind through the silence of the night, a long, deep mutter, then a rising howl, and then the sad moan in which it died away. Again and again it sounded, the whole air throbbing with it, a strident, wild and menacing sound. The baronet caught me by the sleeve.

'Good heavens, what's that, Watson?'

'That's my sleeve,' I said. 'The villagers call it an Eric.'

'Eric?'

'Yes, the homosexual Hound of the Baskervilles is called an Eric — Eric of the Baskervilles.'

'Tell me, Watson, what do you say it is?'

'They say it is a cry of the queer Hound of the Baskervilles who roamed the moor. The hound was called Eric.'

'A supernatural hound it was,' he said at last, 'but it seemed to come from miles away over yonder. I think it needs a vet.'

'It's hard to say from whence it came.'

'No, it isn't; it's quite easy. It rose and fell with the wind. Isn't that the direction of the Great Grimpen Mire?'

'Well, it was up there yesterday,' I replied.

'Come now, Watson, didn't you think yourself that it was the cry of a queer ghostly hound or an Eric?'

'No, no, it was a flesh-and-blood hound; it wasn't a queer hound nor an Eric,' I argued.

'You don't believe it, do you Watson? It was one thing to laugh about in London but it's another to stand in the darkness of the moor and hear such a cry as that. That sound seemed to freeze my very blood. Feel my hand!'

It was as cold as a block of marble.

'Ah, you need a hot bath,' I advised.

'No, we are after a convict and a queer ghostly hound and an Eric. If we shoot him we'll mince him.'

We set out onto the dark and desolate moor. It was strange to see this single candle burning there in the middle of the moor with no sign of life near it – just one straight yellow flame and the gleam of the rock on each side of it.

Over the rocks where the candle burnt was thrust an evil yellow face, a terrible animal face; it looked like Frank Bruno's face upside down, all seamed and scored with vile passions.

'It's an Eric,' I screamed.

We followed him forward, sideways and backward shouting, 'Out of my way, I am holding a pistol and a flask of brandy. The choice is yours. Stop or I will drain this brandy.'

The light reflected his small cunning eyes, which appeared like those of a crafty and savage animal who had heard the steps of hunters.

'Stop! It's nearly Christmas,' I cried.

Our man was running at great speed in the direction

of away. I didn't want to shoot an unarmed man who was running away for Christmas. That's what I'll tell the police. Was he an Eric?'

We ran and ran until we were completely blown, and the space between us grew even wider. Finally we stopped and sat panting on two rocks, while we watched him disappear in the distance. As we did he turned and watched us disappear in the distance.

I wished to go in that direction to search the High Tor where I tort I saw a puddy tat but it was useless: the puddy tat had also run away for Christmas.

Neither one leg nor three is the correct amount for a fully equipped dog.

CHAPTER X

Extract From the Diary of Dr Watson

SIR HENRY was obsessed with impending danger. I felt myself and I felt an impending danger. I have with my own ears heard the sound which resembled the distant baying of a homosexual hound – or an Eric. A spectral hound which leaves a single footprint – perhaps it was one-legged. Whatever it was, it would be easy to identify with one leg. I, myself, had a three-legged dog. His name was Rover but, alas, when he barked he fell over. In fact, at night I have twice heard the creature crying out upon the moor.

'Shut up,' I said. 'There are people down here trying to sleep.'

I could see on the High Tor, Hi Tor I saw a puddy tat. Was it a cat or was it an Eric or was it a one-legged Eric? A stranger then is still dogging us just as a stranger had dogged us in London. We had never shaken him off. I wouldn't like to shake him off.

Sir Henry's nerve had been badly shaken by the sound of the one-legged Eric on the moor.

We had a small scene that morning after breakfast.

Barrymore asked if he could speak with Sir Henry and they were closeted in the billiard room. Sitting outside, I heard them playing a few strokes of snooker and then there seemed to be a row. Then I heard Sir Henry break his cue over Barrymore's head. Barrymore considered he had a grievance.

'I'm a better snooker player than him,' said Barrymore, the blood running down his head.

The butler was standing, very pale but very collected, before us. 'At the same time, I was very much surprised when I heard you two gentlemen come back this morning and learnt that you had been chasing Selden, the Notting Hill murderer,' said he.

'The man is a public danger,' said Baskerville. 'Look at Mr Stapleton's house for example, with no one but himself to defend it. There is no safety for anyone until he is under lock and key by Christmas.'

'Well, sir, he has stopped murdering people. In a few days necessary arrangements will be made and he will be on his way to South America to become a Nazi. For God's sake, don't stop him.'

'But how about the chance of his murdering someone up before he goes?'

'We have provided him a place in the Cambridge Rowing Eleven. It's very hard to commit murder when you're rowing,' said Barrymore.

'All right, then,' said Sir Henry. 'Well, Barrymore –'

'God bless you, sir.' So grateful was he that Barrymore seemed keen to offer us some further information. I've never breathed a word about this yet to a mortal man. It's about poor Sir Charles's death.'

Sir Henry and I were both on our feet.

'Do you know how he died?'

'Some say it was an Eric; some say a homosexual hound. That evening he was to meet a woman.'

'To meet a woman! And the woman's name?'

'I can't give you the name, sir, but she was rhesus negative and her initials were L.L.

'Sir Charles had a letter that morning. It was from Coombe Tracey, and it was addressed in a woman's hand. Only a few weeks ago, after his death, my wife was cleaning out Sir Charles's study and she found the ashes of a burnt letter in the back of the grate. But one little slip, the end of a page, hung together. And it ended: "Please, please, as you are a gentleman, burn this letter, and be at the gate by ten o'clock." Beneath it were signed the initials L.L.'

'Have you got that slip?'

'No, sir, it crumbled to bits and the cat ate it.'

'You mean it might injure his reputation?'

'No, sir, he hasn't got one.'

The answer to the initials L.L. came from Dr Mortimer.

'There are a few gypsies and there is Laura Lyons, blood group rhesus negative. She married an artist named Lyons who came sketching on the moor. Her father refused to have anything to do with her because she had married a Jew without his consent, and perhaps for one or two other reasons as well, and the young girl had a pretty bad time.'

'How did she live?'

'Frugally. Her story got about and several people

did something to enable her to earn an honest living. Stapleton did, for one, and Sir Charles another. I gave her a trifle myself, and she ate it.'

Mortimer wanted to know the object of our enquiries but I managed to quieten him with an oven-ready chicken.

Before we sought out Laura Lyons, the opportunity presented itself to question Barrymore further. The possibility remained that Selden, the Notting Hill murderer, might have had a hand in Sir Charles' demise.

'Did you see your wife's brother on the night of Sir Charles' death?' I asked.

'No, sir, but the food was gone when next I went that way. I think, sir, he has stopped murdering people.'

'Then he was certainly there?'

'Well, sir, everybody has to be somewhere but it could be, sir, that it was the other man who took it.'

'You know that there is another man, then?' asked Sir Henry.

'Yes, sir; there is another man upon the moor.'

'Have you seen him?'

'Yes, sir. He's a queer fellow. I tell you straight, sir, that I don't like queers on the moor.'

'Now listen, Barrymore, tell me frankly what it is that you don't like.'

'Spinach, sir.'

'But what is it that alarms you?'

'All those noises on the moor at night. There are murderers, homosexual hounds, Erics, puddy tat, queers, and Christmas three weeks away. There is not a man who would cross the moor after sundown if he was paid

'Seldon was holding up people and robbing them of their life's savings.'

for it. Selden was holding up people and robbing them of their life's savings.'

'Where did you say he lived?'

'Among the old houses on the hillside – the stone huts where the old folk used to live.'

'And how about his food?'

'Oh, he does McDonald's and chips and he goes to a supermarket.'

'Very good, Barrymore, we may talk further of this some other time. Merry Christmas,' said Sir Henry.

'Christmas is in three months' time, sir.'

'Yes, I don't like to wait until the last minute.'

What passion or hatred can it be that leads a man to a McDonald's and a milkshake? How could he face up to living in a place with packs of Erics about? And who was this mysterious 'other' man most recently seen out upon the moor?

'I thought she had fainted but she recovered herself with a supreme effort by doing a backward somersault into the upright position.'

CHAPTER XI

The Man on the Tor

THE TIME when these strange events began to move swiftly towards their terrible conclusion was too swift for me to keep up with. I had established two facts of great importance: that Mrs Lyons, blood group rhesus negative, had written to Sir Charles Baskerville, blood group G, and they made an appointment to meet the hour that he met his death. Of course, when she arrived he wasn't there.

When we all sat down to breakfast the next morning, the absence of Sir Charles Baskerville was entirely due to his recent death.

'Shall we have two minutes' silence?' said Sir Henry.

This we did and I whistled the 'Dead March'.

After breakfast we paid a visit to the aforementioned Laura Lyons. My first impression of Mrs Lyons, blood group rhesus negative, was a pleasant smile of welcome.

'I had the pleasure,' said I, 'of knowing your father.' It was a clumsy introduction, and the lady made me feel it, so I felt it. 'Did you correspond with Sir Charles?'

'I certainly wrote to him once or twice to acknowledge his kindness and generosity,' she said.

'Did he know you were blood group rhesus negative? Surely your memory deceives you,' said I. 'I could even quote a passage of your letter. It ran, "Please, please, as you are a gentleman, burn this letter, and be at the gate by ten o'clock with your cheque book." '

I thought that she had fainted, but she recovered herself with a supreme effort by doing a backward somersault into the upright position.

'Do you think a woman could go alone at that hour to a bachelor's house? I never got there.'

'Why not?'

'Something intervened to prevent my going.'

'What was that?'

'An elephant fell on me. I tell you, if you heard anything of my unhappy history you know that I made a rash marriage for which I have reason to regret. If it had been rasher, it would have been bacon.'

'Then how is it that you did not go?'

'I keep telling you an elephant fell on me. So I should have met with him the following day had I not seen his death in the paper next morning.'

'He died in a newspaper?'

'Yes, the *Mirror*.'

'What a terrible paper to die in.'

Sir Henry was sitting in the lounge when Barrymore announced, 'Sir Henry, the Berlin Philharmonic have arrived.'

'Well, show them in and tell them to start playing "The Valkyries".'

Mr Frankland, the gentleman who took such great

delight in closing down the countryside to members of the general public had also come to call.

'Good day, Dr Watson,' said he.

'Good morning, you miserable bastard,' I said.

'It is a great day for me, sir – one of the red-letter days of my life. I have established a right of way through the centre of old Middleton's park, slap across it, sir, within a hundred yards of his own front door. What do you think of that? Wait a moment, Dr Watson. Do my eyes deceive me, or is there something moving upon that hillside?'

I could distinctly see a small dark dot against the dull green and grey.

'Come, sir, come!' cried Frankland, rushing upstairs. 'You will see with your own eyes and judge for yourself.'

The telescope, a formidable instrument mounted upon a tripod, stood upon the flat leads of the house. Sure enough, a small urchin with a little bundle upon his shoulder toiled slowly up the hill. He looked as though he had bubonic plague. When he reached the crest I saw the ragged, uncouth figure outlined for an instant against the cold blue sky. He looked round him with a furtive and stealthy air. Then he vanished over the hill. I resolved to investigate this mysterious figure at my earliest opportunity.

The sun was sinking when I reached the summit of High Tor. There wasn't a puddy tat in sight. One great grey bird soared aloft in the blue heaven. He and I seemed to be the only living things between the sky and the desert beneath it.

I approached the hut, walking as warily as Stapleton

'I turned around and a shadow fell across the opening of the hut.'

would do. I was by myself but the place had indeed been used as a habitation. Throwing aside my cigarette, I closed my hand upon the butt of my revolver and, walking swiftly to the door, I said, 'Come out or I will come in and kill you. Now you wouldn't like that.' I went inside and fired my pistol and shouted, 'I know you're outside because you're not inside. If you give yourself up I'll give you a chocolate and a ticket to the opera. Now listen, hands up before Christmas and a Happy New Year.'

I looked under every rock outcrop and there was nothing. All I got was a pain in the back. Then, as I returned to the hut, I heard the sharp clink of a boot striking upon a stone. Then another and yet another, coming nearer and nearer. I shrank back into the darkest corner, cocked my pistol, determined not to be discovered. I turned around and a shadow fell across the opening of the hut.

'It is a lovely evening, my dear Watson,' said a well-known voice. 'I really think that you will be more comfortable outside than in.'

'There was a loud bang and I shot myself in the foot.'

CHAPTER XII

Death on the Moor

OR A moment I sat breathless. That cold, incisive, ironical voice could belong to but one man in all the world.

'Holmes!' I cried. 'Holmes! Holmes! Holmes!'

'There's only one of me, Watson. Come out,' he said, 'and please be careful with the revolver.'

There was a loud bang and I shot myself in the foot.

'You see there beside the path?' said Holmes. 'You threw the cigarette down at the supreme moment when you charged into the hut to find it empty.'

'Exactly.'

He was still wearing one brown boot and one black one, silly bugger.

'You saw me, perhaps, on the night of the convict hunt, when I was so imprudent as to allow the moon to rise behind me?'

'Not at all. We ran our arses ragged chasing that devil Selden but saw nothing of you. You, then, are the "other" man on the moor! But why keep me in the dark, Holmes?'

'It saves electricity, Watson.'

* * *

'Excuse me, sir,' said Barrymore. 'The Berlin Philharmonic have finished "The Valkyries".'

'Then tell them to play some extracts by Wagner and when finish they can go back to Germany.'

A terrible scream – a prolonged yell of horror and anguish – burst out of the silence of the moor. That frightful cry turned the blood to ice in my veins.

'Agggggggg!!'

'Good God, what is it? What does it mean?' What is the meaning of Agggggggg?' I cried.

Holmes sprang to his feet. I saw his dark, athletic outline at the door of the hut, his shoulders stooping, his head thrust forward, his face peering into the darkness. He walked into a rock.

'What is it?' Holmes whispered. 'Is it an Eric or a queer hound of the Baskervilles? Where is it, Watson?'

'There, I think.' I pointed into the darkness. 'No, there! No, there! No, there!' So I went there and there and there and Holmes went there and there and there, too.

Again, an agonised cry swept through the silent night. Whatever it was sounded as though it had got its balls caught in a rat trap.

'The hound!' cried Holmes. 'Come, Watson, come! Great heavens, if we are too late!'

I saw Holmes put his hand to his forehead. It was still there. 'He has beaten us, Watson. We are too late.'

'No, no, surely not!'

'Fool that I was to hold my hand. And you, Watson, see what comes of abandoning your charge. But, by heaven, if the worst has happened, we'll avenge him. Can you see anything?'

'Yes, anything.'

'That's no bloody good. Hark! Hark!'

'I can't see anything and I am harking as much as I can.'

A low moan had fallen upon our ears. There it was again upon our left! On the boulder strewn hillside was spread-eagled some dark, irregular object. As we ran towards it the vague outline hardened into a definite shape. It was a prostrate man face downward upon the ground, the head doubled under him at a horrible angle, the shoulders rounded, and the body hunched together as if in the act of throwing a somersault. So grotesque was that attitude that I could not for the instant realise that that moan had been the passing of his soul. Not a whisper, not a rustle, rose now from the dark figure over which we stooped. Holmes laid his hand upon him, and held it up again, with an exclamation of horror. 'Mark my words, Watson,' said Holmes. 'This is the work of that villain Stapleton.'

'Why should we not seize them at once?' I asked.

'Our case is not complete. The fellow is wary and cunning to the last degree.'

'We must send for help, Holmes! We cannot carry the body all the way to the Hall. Let's put a rock on it so that the cat doesn't get him.'

We put our hands in the dead man's pocket and it came to thirty shillings in loose change. He was not only dead but also skint.

'The man has a beard!' cried Holmes.

'A beard?'

'It is not Sir Henry – it is . . . why, it is my neighbour, Selden, the Notting Hill murderer, and he has apparently stopped murdering.'

The Notting Hill murderer had Sir Henry's old wardrobe and Barrymore had passed it on in order to disguise Selden's escape.

'These clothes have been the cause of the poor fellow's death. The homosexual Hound of the Baskervilles recognised the smell as belonging to Sir Henry. By his cries he must have run a long way after he knew the homosexual hound was on his track.'

'How did he die?'

'Well, he ran like fuck, when he saw what he thought was an Eric or a homosexual hound and had a heart attack.'

'Well, then, why should this hound be loose tonight? It would normally not run loose upon the moor except to kill a policeman, a farmer or a duck. Stapleton would not let it go unless he had reason to think that Sir Henry would be there.'

Quack! Quack! Stop that duck!

'Halloa, Watson, what's this? It is Stapleton himself. Not a word to show your suspicions.'

A figure was approaching us over the moor. I saw the dull red glow of a cigar. Though it was midnight, he carried a butterfly net. It was a disguise.

'Why, Dr Watson, that's not you is it? You are the last man that I expected to see,' said Stapleton.

'Well, I dearly hope I am not.'

'Is somebody hurt? Don't tell me it's our friend Sir Henry.'

'All right then, I won't tell you.'

He hurried past me and stooped over the dead man. I heard a sharp intake of his breath and the cigar fell from his fingers.

'Who is this?'

'It is Selden, the Notting Hill murderer,' I informed him.

Stapleton turned a ghastly face upon us, but by a supreme effort he had overcome his amazement and his disappointment.

'Dear me! What a horrible affair! How did he die?'

'Death,' said Holmes.

'So death finally killed him.'

'He appears to have broken his neck by falling over these rocks. My friend and I were strolling on the moor when we heard a cry,' I said.

'I also heard a cry. That's what brought me out. I was uneasy about Sir Henry,' said Stapleton.

'Why Sir Henry in particular?' I could not help asking.

Holmes blurted out, 'The bloody fool.'

'Because I had suggested he come over. When he did not come I was surprised, and I naturally became alarmed for his safety when I heard cries upon the moor. By the way –' his eyes darted again from my face to Holmes's '– did you hear anything else besides a cry?'

'No, of course not. Did you?' I answered.

'No.'

'What do you mean then?'

'I mean no. I hope your visit has cast some light upon those occurrences, whether it was an Eric or a homosexual hound.'

Holmes shrugged his shoulders. 'One cannot always have the success for which one hopes.'

My friend spoke in his frankest and most unconcerned manner. Stapleton still looked hard at him. Then he turned to me.

'I would suggest carrying this poor fellow to my house, but it would give my sister such a fright that I do not feel justified in doing it. I think if we put something over his face he will be safe until morning.'

So we put another rock over his face.

Holmes and I set off for Baskerville Hall, leaving the naturalist to return alone. Looking back we saw the figure moving slowly away over the broad moor, and behind him that one black smudge on the silvered slope which showed where the man was lying who had come so horribly to his end.

'We're at close grips at last,' said Holmes.

'I am sorry that he has seen you, Holmes.'

'And so was I at first. But there was no getting out of it.'

'Why should we not arrest him at once and not Doris Stokes?'

'*Doris Stokes???!!!* We should be laughed out of court if we came with such a story and such evidence. We might as well blame her for the Boer War.'

'Who was responsible for the Boer War?'

'Mrs Doris Grub, 33 Wellington Street, Hackney.'

'How do you propose to confront her?'

'I have great hopes of what Mrs Laura Lyons may do for us tomorrow. And now we are late for dinner. I think that we are both ready for sustenance.'

'. . . she wept bitterly in her apron so we put her through
the mangle.'

CHAPTER XIII
Fixing the Nets

SIR HENRY was more than pleased and surprised to see Sherlock Holmes. He did raise his eyebrows, where they stuck, however, when he heard that my friend had neither any luggage nor any explanations for its absence. But first I had the unpleasant duty of breaking the news of the death of Selden the Notting Hill murderer to Barrymore and his wife. To him it may have been an unmitigated relief, but she wept bitterly in her apron so we put her through the mangle.

'Don't worry,' said Holmes. 'He is lying out on the moor with a rock on him. You can visit him whenever you like. He's not going far.'

Sir Henry opened his eyes. 'How did he come to die?'

'The poor wretch was dressed in your clothes. I fear your servant who gave them to him may get into trouble with the police.'

'But how about the case?' asked Sir Henry. 'Have you found the guilty person? And have you found my other boots?'

'We've had one experience, as Watson has no doubt told you. We heard one of the Erics on the moor.'

He stopped suddenly and stared fixedly up over my

head into the air. The lamp beat upon his face, and so intent was his gaze and so still that it might have been that of a clear-cut classical statue.

I could see as he looked down that he was repressing some internal emotion. His features were still composed, but his eyes shone with amused exultation.

'Excuse the admiration of a connoisseur,' said Holmes, as he waved his hand towards the line of portraits which covered the opposite wall. 'Watson won't allow that I know anything of art but that is because he is entirely ignorant. That stout gentleman with the wig ought to be a Reynolds. They are all family portraits, I presume? Do you know the names? And this Cavalier opposite to me – the one with the black velvet and lace?'

'Ah, you have a right to know about him. That is the cause of all the mischief, the wicked Hugo the shit, who started the homosexual Hound of the Baskervilles.'

Holmes stood on a chair and went through it. He held the light up against the time-stained portrait on the wall.

'Good heavens!' I cried, in amazement.

The face of Stapleton had sprung out of the canvas. Holmes burst into one of his rare fits of laughter as he turned away from the picture.

'If only he knew how ridiculous he looked with a brown nose.'

Finale

'Y ES, WE should have a full day today,' Holmes remarked, smothering his nose with a pinch of snuff. If only he knew how ridiculous he looked with a brown nose.

'I have sent a report from Grimpen to Princetown as to the death of Selden. I think I can promise that none of you will be troubled in the matter of his death, although there might be an inquiry about the rock on his face and body. You are engaged, as I understand, to dine with our friends the Stapletons tonight.'

'Yes,' replied Sir Henry. 'I hope that you will come also.'

'I fear that Watson and I must go to London.'

Sir Henry's face dropped and hit the floor.

'My dear fellow,' said Holmes, 'you must trust me implicitly and do exactly what I tell you. We will drive in to Coombe Tracey, but Watson will leave his things as a pledge that he will come back. Watson, you will send a note to Stapleton to tell him that you regret that you cannot come.'

'All right then, I will go on my own,' said Sir Henry. 'Fuck it.'

'One more direction!' Holmes instructed our host. 'I

wish you to drive to Merripit House. Send back your trap, however, and let them know that you intend to walk home.'

'Bloody hell! But that is the very thing which you have so often cautioned me not to do.'

'This time you will do it with safety.'

'Then I will do it.'

'Good boy,' said Holmes, patting his head and giving him a lump of sugar.

'Good doggy,' I said, trying to pat him.

'And, as you value your life, do not go across the moor in any direction save along the straight path. Good boy,' Holmes said, patting him and giving him another lump of sugar.

We said goodbye to our rueful friend. I left him chewing a sugar lump, cocking his leg and peeing against a tree. And after a couple of hours we were at the station of Coombe Tracey. A small boy was waiting on the platform.

'Any orders, sir?'

'Yes, you will take this train to town, Cartwright. The moment you arrive you will seek out Inspector Lestrade of Scotland Yard. You will give him this letter and ask him to wire his reply to me at this station immediately.'

It was later that morning when the telegram arrived, which Holmes handed to me. It ran:

> WIRE RECEIVED. PROCEED. COMING DOWN
> WITH UNSIGNED WARRANT AND CHANGE OF
> UNDERWEAR. ARRIVE FIVE-FORTY.
>   LESTRADE.

'Now we must visit Mrs Laura Lyons,' Holmes announced.

Mrs Laura Lyons, blood group rhesus negative, was in her office, and Sherlock Holmes opened the interview.

'I am investigating the circumstances which attended the death of the late Sir Charles Baskerville. Dr Watson said in a previous interview you withheld information.'

'What have I withheld?' she asked defiantly.

'You confessed that you asked Sir Charles to be at the gate at ten o'clock. You have withheld the connection.'

'There is no connection.'

'In that case I wish to be perfectly frank with you, Mrs Lyons. We regard this case as one of murder, and the evidence may implicate not only your friend, Mr Stapleton, but his wife as well.'

The lady sprang from her chair and hit the wall opposite.

'His wife!' she cried.

'The fact is no longer a secret. The person who has passed for his sister is really his wife. Stapleton himself is an illegitimate descendant of Hugo the Shit and will step forward to inherit the Baskerville fortune once the rightful heir is out of the way.'

Sherlock Holmes shrugged his shoulders. A lot of bloody good it did.

'One thing I swear to you is that when I wrote that letter I never dreamt of any harm to the old gentleman,' said Mrs Lyons.

She did a quick back somersault and landed on her feet.

'I entirely believe you, madam,' said Sherlock Holmes. 'I presume you received help from Sir Charles for the legal expenses in connection with your divorce. What persuaded you from keeping the appointment?'

'An elephant fell on me,' she said. 'He frightened me into remaining silent.'

'But you had your suspicions?'

'Yes, Doris Stokes.'

She held up a cardboard cutout of Tutankhamen. Holmes put it under his arm.

The London express came roaring into the station and crashed into the buffer with its bumpers. A small, wiry bulldog of a man was hurled on the platform from the first-class carriage. We all three shook hands. I shook two of his; he shook one of mine.

'Anything good?' asked Inspector Lestrade.

'Yes, there's a marmalade fair in the village.'

'Lestrade got into a hollow. It gradually filled with fog, obscuring him completely.'

THE END

CHAPTER XIV

The Hound of the Baskervilles

ONE OF Sherlock Holmes's defects is that all of the plans he makes he neglects to tell anybody about. I had no idea what the hell was going on.

'Are you armed, Lestrade?'

The little detective smiled. 'As long as I have my trousers, I have something in it: a nine-millimetre Colt automatic.'

'Good! My friend and I are also ready for emergencies. I have a pint hip flask of Napoleon brandy.'

'You are mighty close about this affair, Holmes. What's the game now?' I asked.

'I will find the murderer and post him to the police for Christmas. There is Merripit House and the end of our journey. I must request you to walk on tiptoe and not to talk above a whisper. This will do,' said he. 'Get into this hollow, Lestrade.'

Lestrade gradually got into a hollow. It gradually filled with fog, obscuring him completely.

'Can you tell the position of the rooms?' asked Holmes.

'Yes, nor'west,' I said.

'What are those latticed windows at this end?'

'I think they are the kitchen windows.'

'And the one beyond, which shines so brightly?'

'That is certainly the dining room.'

'The blinds are up. You know the lie of the land best. Creep forward and see what they are doing!'

There were only two men in the room, Sir Henry and Stapleton. They sat with their profiles towards me on either side of the round table. Both of them were smoking cigars, and coffee and wine were in front of them. Stapleton was talking with animation but Sir Henry looked pale and distrait.

As I watched them, Stapleton rose and left the room, while Sir Henry filled his glass again and leant back in his chair, puffing at his cigar. I heard the creak of a door and the crisp sound of boots upon gravel. Looking over, I saw the naturalist pause at the door of an outhouse in the corner of the orchard. A key turned in a lock, and as he passed in there was a curious scuffling noise from within. He was only a minute or so inside, and then I heard the key turn once more, and he passed me and re-entered the house.

'You say, Watson, that the lady is not there?' Holmes asked.

'No. Perhaps she's cooking.'

'But there is no light in any other room, including the kitchen?'

'Perhaps she's cooking in Braille.'

The fog bank fell back until we were half a mile from the house, and still that dense white sea, with the moon silvering its upper edge, swept slowly and inexorably on. Lestrade was absolutely forgotten in that hole. We watched as Sir Henry left Merripit House to begin his long, lonely walk home.

'Hist!' cried Holmes, and I heard the sharp click of a cocking pistol. 'Look out! It's coming!'

I was at Holmes's elbow, and I glanced for an instant at his face. It was pale and exultant, his eyes shining brightly in the moonlight. But then they started forward in a rigid, fixed stare, and his lips parted in amazement. At the same instant Lestrade gave a yell of terror and threw himself downward upon the ground. I sprang to my feet, my inert hand grasping my pistol, my mind paralysed by the dreadful shape that had sprung out upon us from the shadows of the fog. A homosexual hound it was, an enormous coal-black hound, but not such a hound as mortal eyes have ever seen. Fire burst from its open mouth, its eyes glowed with smouldering flames, its muzzle and hackles and dewlap were outlined in the flickering flame. Never in the delirious dream of a disordered brain could anything more savage, more appalling, more hellish, be conceived than that dark form and savage face which broke upon us out of the wall of fog.

'Oh nice doggy, doggy here.' I tried to offer him a biscuit.

Then Holmes and I both fired together, and the creature gave a hideous howl, which showed that one at least

'*"Oh nice doggy, doggy here." I tried to offer him a biscuit.*'

had hit him. He did not pause, however, but bounded onward. Far away on the path we saw Sir Henry looking back, his face white in the moonlight, his hands raised in horror, glaring helplessly at the frightful thing that was hunting him down. 'Down, Fido,' he gasped, but Fido did not go down. Fido sprang at his throat. But the next instant Holmes had emptied five chambers of his revolver into the creature's flank. With a last howl of agony and a vicious snap in the air, it rolled upon its back, and then fell limp upon its side. I stooped, panting, and pressed my pistol to the dreadful, shimmering head, but it was useless to press the trigger. The giant homosexual hound lay dead.

Lestrade thrust his brandy flask between the baronet's teeth.

'My God!' Sir Henry whispered. 'What was it? What, in heaven's name, was it?' he said, swallowing.

'It's a Napoleon brandy, '89,' said Lestrade.

'It's a large Eric,' I said. 'Yes, it's dead. We have laid the family ghost once and for ever.' I placed my hand upon the glowing muzzle, and as I held them up my own fingers smouldered and gleamed in the darkness.

'Phosphorus,' I said.

The dog had a name on his collar, 'Tiddles'.

'You saved my life, Holmes,' said the baronet.

'We all make mistakes,' said Holmes. 'Are you strong enough to stand?'

'Give me another mouthful of that brandy, and I shall be able to stand anything.' He drank the bottle and collapsed.

He tried to stagger to his feet and passed out, but he

was still ghastly pale and trembling in every limb. We helped him to a rock. He wouldn't eat it.

At that moment there came a horrific scream and a hissing, gurgling, squelching sound from the direction of the Grimpen Mire. Stapleton, rushing to view the fiendish work of his hideous hound had met his fate, sinking into the foul depths of the bog to join the unfortunate pony, the postman and the milkman.

Original Rewrite of
Sir Arthur Conan Doyle

E ALL drove to Stapleton's for the denouement. There was nobody in. We went into a room that had been fashioned into a small museum, and the walls were lined by glass-topped cases full of that collection of butterflies and moths the formation of which had been the relaxation of this complex and dangerous man. In the centre of this room there was an upright beam, which had been placed at some period as a support for the old worm-eaten balk of timber which spanned the roof. To this post a figure was tied, so swathed and muffled in the sheets which had been used to secure it that one could not for the moment tell whether it was that of a man or woman. One towel passed round the throat, and was secured at the back of the pillar. Another covered the lower part of the face and over it two dark eyes – eyes full of grief and shame and a dreadful questioning – stared back at us, a moustache pencilled under her nose. In a minute we had torn off the gag, unswathed the bonds, and Mrs Stapleton sank upon the floor in front of us and her beautiful head fell forward. It went thud as it hit the floor.

'The brute!' cried Holmes. 'Here, Lestrade, your flask! Put her in the chair! She has fainted from ill usage, housework and laundry. I will just squeeze them while she's unconscious.'

She opened her eyes again. 'Is he safe?' she asked. 'Has he escaped?'

'He cannot escape us, madam.'

'No, no, I did not mean my husband. Is Sir Henry safe?'

'Yes, and the homosexual hound is dead.'

She gave a long sigh of satisfaction. 'Thank God! Thank God! Oh, this villain! See how he has treated me!'

Kinky, eh?

We saw with horror that her arms were tattooed with the winning numbers of the National Lottery and she had won millions.

'To hell with Sir Henry! I don't need him and I don't need anybody,' she cried.

'Marry me,' said Holmes. And they lived happily ever after.

Somewhere in the heart of the Grimpen Mire, down in the foul slime of the huge morass that had sucked Stapleton in, this cold and cruel-hearted man is for ever buried.

'Excuse me, sir, the Berlin Philharmonic have finished the Wagner selection.'

'Go and tell them to start playing World War One with my compliments.'

Quack! Quack! Stop that duck!

HOLMES

WATSON

THE END